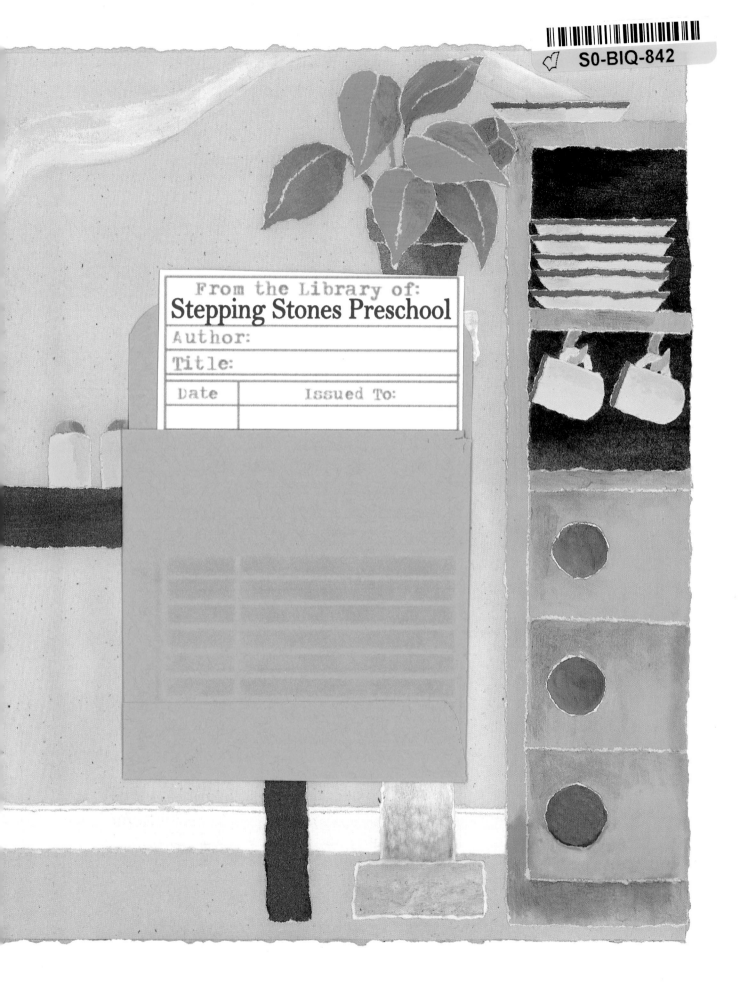

For Shirin, Billy and Cameron
L.J.
For my brother Marc –
who's always up to
something!
T.L.

Text copyright © 1997 by Linda Jennings
Pictures copyright © 1997 by Tanya Linch
All rights reserved
First published in England by Magi Publications, 1997
Printed and bound in Belgium by Proost NV, Turnhout
First American edition, 1997

Library of Congress Cataloging-in-Publication Data
Jennings, Linda.
Easy peasy! / Linda Jennings ; pictures by Tanya Linch.
p.   cm.
Summary: By jumping up onto higher and higher objects,
Kitty manages to reach a tempting plate of fish.
    ISBN 0-374-31949-9
    1. Cats—Juvenile fiction. [1. Cats—Fiction.]
    I. Linch, Tanya, ill. II. Title.
    PZ10.3. J429Eas   1997
    [E]—dc20   96-27661

Easy Peasy!

by **Linda Jennings**

Pictures by **Tanya Linch**

Farrar, Straus and Giroux

New York

Kitty woke up hungry.
Something was making
her nose twitch.
What was that
delicious smell?

She jumped off the chair and raced across the hall into the kitchen.

Kitty looked in her bowl,
but there was no food in it.
So where was the smell
coming from?
Then she saw . . .

. . . a plate of fish,
right on top of the kitchen cupboard,
just waiting for a hungry kitten.

"But I'm down here,
and it's up there," she said sadly.
What should she do?

"Maybe if I wait here, someone will come along
and get it down for me," thought Kitty.
She curled up in her basket
and shut her eyes, but it was no use.
She just couldn't
forget about the fish.

What should she do?
"*I* know!" cried Kitty.
"It's easy peasy!"

Kitty jumped onto the bucket.
She was higher now,
but she still couldn't reach
the top of the cupboard.

What should she do?
"*I* know," cried Kitty.
"It's easy peasy!"

Kitty jumped onto the stool.
Her mouth watered.
But she still couldn't reach
the top of the cupboard.

What should she do?
"*I* know!" cried Kitty.
"It's easy peasy!"

Kitty jumped onto the table,
and nearly slid off the end.
Her tummy rumbled.
But she still couldn't reach
the top of the cupboard.

What should she do?
"*I* know," cried Kitty.
"It's easy peasy!"

Kitty jumped from the table
to the plant stand.
She was getting hungrier
by the minute!
And she was almost
there!

"It's *really* easy peasy now!" cried Kitty.
She jumped from the plant stand
to the top of the cabinet . . .

. . . and
landed on
the plate!
The plate slid . . .

. . . off the edge,
and fell down
down
down
to the floor,
just as Pup
was coming into the kitchen . . .

. . . and with a
slurp and a gulp,
he ate the fish
in one bite!

"Serves you right for being so greedy,"
said Mouse.
But Kitty had another worry . . .

How was she going to get
down again?
"*That* won't be easy peasy at all!"
said Mouse.